Other books in the
Little Polar Bear series

LITTLE POLAR BEAR
·
AHOY THERE, LITTLE POLAR BEAR
·
LITTLE POLAR BEAR FINDS A FRIEND
·
LITTLE POLAR BEAR, TAKE ME HOME!
·
LITTLE POLAR BEAR AND THE BRAVE LITTLE HARE

For FZ

Copyright © 1999 by Nord-Süd Verlag AG, Gossau Zürich, Switzerland
First published in Switzerland under the title *Kleiner Eisbär lass mich nicht allein!*
English translation copyright © 1999 by North-South Books Inc.

First published in the United States, Great Britain, Canada,
Australia, and New Zealand in 1999 by North-South Books,
an imprint of Nord-Süd Verlag AG, Gossau Zürich, Switzerland.

Distributed in the United States by North-South Books Inc., New York.

Library of Congress Cataloging-in-Publication Data is available.
A CIP catalogue record for this book is available from The British Library.
ISBN 0-7358-1154-7 (TRADE BINDING)
1 3 5 7 9 TB 10 8 6 4 2
ISBN 0-7358-1155-5 (LIBRARY BINDING)
1 3 5 7 9 LB 10 8 6 4 2
Printed in Belgium

For more information about our books, and the authors and artists
who create them, visit our web site: www.northsouth.com

Little Polar Bear
and the Husky Pup

Written and Illustrated by
Hans de Beer

Translated by Rosemary Lanning

North-South Books
New York / London

Lars, the Little Polar Bear, lived at the North Pole, where there are no trees or flowers, just ice and snow. Lars didn't mind. He loved to go for long walks across the ice, always wondering what he might find behind the next snow hill.

One day Lars walked even farther than usual, and he was very hungry. He lifted his nose and sniffed. There was a delicious smell in the air, but he didn't know what it was.

The delicious smell came from an igloo. That meant there were people! Lars's father had warned him to stay away from people. "They're dangerous!" he always said.

But the smell from the igloo was so tempting that Lars couldn't resist. He crawled closer, keeping well away from a team of sled dogs, who seemed to be fast asleep. Suddenly there was a growl. The huskies jumped up and strained at their leashes. The leashes snapped, and the whole team rushed at Lars, barking furiously.

Lars was lucky he had a head start. When the dogs saw
they would never catch up with him, they lost interest and
turned back. At last Lars could stop and catch his breath.
He crawled into an ice cave and went to sleep.

He was woken by a strange noise. It sounded like a
whimper, but Lars couldn't see where it came from.
He walked over to a deep crack in the ice and peered down.
There sat a sad little husky. Although the other dogs had
given him a fright, he felt sorry for this little one.

"Don't be frightened," said Lars. "I'll help you!"

Lars started to push snow into the hole. He worked and
worked until the pile of snow was big enough to let the little
dog climb all the way out. But as soon as the puppy was back
on firm ground he began to growl.

"Hey! I just helped you!" said Lars indignantly.

The puppy barked.

How ungrateful! thought Lars. He turned away in disgust, and bounded off towards the sea. The little dog ran after him. Lars ran across the chunks of ice until he had left the puppy far behind. The puppy sat down on a drifting piece of ice and howled pitifully.

"I would gladly help," Lars shouted to the puppy, "but I don't want to be growled at!"

The little dog looked embarrassed. "I won't growl," he said. "I promise. Please don't leave me!"

So Lars towed the puppy back to shore.

"What's your name?" he asked. "Mine's Lars."

"I'm Floe. Will you take me back to the igloo? I want my mother, and I'm hungry!"

"I'll take you home tomorrow, if it stops snowing," said Lars. "We can wait out the storm here."

Then Lars caught some fish and offered one to Floe, who gobbled it up.

"That wasn't as good as meat," Floe complained.

"You'll have meat again soon," said Lars.

He shovelled snow into a pile and they lay down to sleep behind it, sheltered from the icy wind.

The next morning Lars and Floe set off under a clear
blue sky to find the igloo. But when they got there
the dogs had gone, and snow had covered their tracks.

"I want my mother!" wailed Floe. Then he began
to howl, louder than ever.

This time Lars understood why. He tried to comfort
the little dog. "We'll find her," he said. "Tell me which
way you were heading."

"To the town by the sea, where lots of people live."

"Oh, yes, I know it," said Lars. "Let's go."

The little polar bear and the puppy walked on and on. They didn't stop even when darkness fell. So they didn't see the hunters until it was almost too late! They had to duck down quickly behind some rocks.

The hunters came closer and closer. Suddenly Floe began to growl.

"Shh!" hissed Lars. "You'll give us away!"

But the impetuous puppy jumped up and started barking.

"Huh! It's just a stray dog," said one of the hunters, laughing. Then he and his friends got back on their snowmobiles and drove away.

"Phew! You did the right thing, after all," said Lars, "but I don't think we should go any further tonight. We'll find your mother tomorrow, Floe."

In the morning they walked to the sea. A pair of seals was basking on the shore. Floe charged at them, barking excitedly.

"Stop, Floe! Leave them alone!" shouted Lars, as the seals fled into the water.

Suddenly Floe stopped barking. "Lars! Look at this!" he yapped. He had found an old kayak.

"Kayaks belong to people," said Lars, looking anxious, "and people are dangerous." He sniffed the kayak all over. Then he said, "It's all right. Nobody has used this kayak for a long time. What a good find! Now we can travel twice as fast."

"Paddling a kayak isn't as easy as it looks," said Lars, as they wobbled across the water.

"Never mind," said Floe. "I think we're nearly there. Tonight we'll have meat for supper. Hooray!"

"Listen," said Lars sternly, "you're not to run off after meat! You must stay close to me."

In the twilight, as the kayak slipped silently towards the town, they both began to feel nervous.

"Don't make a sound, Floe," whispered Lars.

And for once Floe kept his mouth shut tight.

But the moment they stepped ashore, Floe cried, "I smell food!" And before Lars could stop him, he was gone!

What was Lars to do? As he stood wondering, he heard a shout: "Stop, thief!" and Floe ran past him with a funny chain hanging from his mouth. Lars ran after him. When they were at a safe distance from the town, Floe stopped and laid the funny chain at Lars's feet.

"That smells good," said Lars.

"Just wait till you taste it!" said Floe. "It's not like fish at all."

But the more Floe ate, the sadder he seemed to be. "Will I ever find my mother?" he said mournfully.

Then he lifted his little head and gave a desperate howl.

There he goes again, thought Lars. What could he do to keep the reckless little creature quiet?

Then Lars heard loud, excited barks. There was no time to run away. Suddenly he was surrounded by dogs, but they didn't hurt him. One of them was Floe's mother. She had heard her puppy howling and rushed to find him.

Floe told his mother how Lars had found him and brought him to the town.

"Thank you, Lars," she said. "Now you must let us take you home."

The two friends hopped onto the dogsled and were whisked away.

"This is more fun than kayaking," said Lars happily.

Lars's parents were amazed to see Lars jump off a dogsled, and even more amazed by the funny chain that Floe laid at their feet.

"Here's something that tastes much better than fish!" he told them.

Then he turned to Lars and said, "I want you to have my collar. It will help you remember me."

The dog team barked a farewell and sped away.

As Floe's sled disappeared over the horizon, Lars put down the collar, raised his head, and howled.

How strange it sounded, and how sad, thought his parents.

After that, Lars was often seen with a smile on his face and a bright red collar around his neck.